Don't count the number of birthdays.
Count how happy you feel. I'm Birthday
Bear, and I'll help make your birthdays
the best ever.

I'm Wish Bear, and if
you wish on my star,
maybe your special dream
will come true.

If you're ever feeling lonely,
just call on me, Friend Bear.
See, I've got a daisy for you
and a daisy for me.

Grr! I'm Grumpy Bear. There's a cloud on
my tummy to show that I take the grouchies
away, so you can be happy again.

I'm Love-a-Lot Bear. I have two
hearts on my tummy. One is for you;
the other is for someone you love.

It's my job to bring you sweet dreams.
I'm Bedtime Bear, and right now I'm a bit
sleepy. Are you sleepy, too?

Now that you know all of us, we hope
that you'll have a special place for us in your
heart, just like we do for you.

With love from all of us,

The Care Bears

Care Bears, Tenderheart Bear, Friend Bear, Grumpy Bear, Birthday Bear, Cheer Bear, Bedtime Bear, Funshine Bear, Love-a-Lot
Bear, Wish Bear and Good Luck Bear are trademarks of American Greetings Corporation.

Library of Congress Cataloging in Publication Data: Hubert, Amelia. Sweet dreams for Sally. SUMMARY: Sally's fear of the dark
keeps her awake at night and makes her grouchy in the morning until Grumpy Bear and Bedtime Bear come to her rescue.
[1. Bedtime—Fiction. 2. Behavior—Fiction 3. Bears—Fiction] I. Cooke, Tom, ill.
II. Title. PZ7.H86314Sw 1982 [E] 82-22332 ISBN: 0-910313-01-6
Manufactured in the United States of America.   3 4 5 6 7 8 9 0

A Tale from the Care Bears

Sweet Dreams for Sally

Story by Amelia Hubert
Pictures by Tom Cooke

Sally lay in bed and looked at the dark. Sally didn't like it.

In the dark the curtains said whisper . . . whisper.

In the dark the window shade said rattle . . . rattle.

In the dark the clock said tic . . . toc.

Sally wondered if something was in her room making those sounds. She started to get a little bit scared.

"I am a big girl now," Sally said to herself. "I will not call my parents. I know that there is nothing to be frightened of. I will shut my eyes, count to ten and go to sleep."

Sally shut her eyes and counted to ten, but it was not easy to get to sleep. She twisted and turned all night long. Sally did not have a good night's sleep.

The next morning Sally felt grouchy when she got up. She was still tired, and she did not feel like going to school.

In the kitchen Sally did not say, "Thank you," when her mother gave her some orange juice.

"Well," said her father. "Did you wake up on the wrong side of the bed this morning?"

"I hardly even slept at all last night, so I don't feel like I woke up at all," said Sally in a cranky voice.

"That's too bad," said her father. "I hope you'll sleep better tonight."

That day in school Sally was so sleepy that she got
five wrong on her spelling test.
She dropped the turtle food all over the floor.

And because she was feeling grumpy,
she had a fight with her best friend, Amy.
"Sally, you are such a
grouch today," Amy said. "I
don't think I want to play
with you after school."

Sally walked home
by herself. She still felt tired,
and now she felt sad
and lonely, too.

When she reached the corner near her house, she heard a gruff voice say, "Hey there, Sally; I wish you were in a better mood. You're feeling so grouchy that you're making my tummy rumble."

"What?" said Sally. She tried to find where the voice was coming from. She looked all around and saw no one. Then she looked up, and there in the branches of a big oak tree was a little blue bear with a frown on his face and a rain cloud on his tummy.

"My goodness," said Sally. "Who are you, and how did you know my name?"

"My name is Grumpy Bear, and I know your name because I know the names of almost everyone who is feeling grumpy. I came to see you because you seem to have a bad case of Grouch-itis. I can tell because it's making my tummy rumble. Listen."

And with that Grumpy Bear floated down from the tree and pointed to the little, blue cloud on his stomach.

Sally put her ear to his tummy, and sure enough, there was a noise coming out of the cloud. It sounded like distant thunder.

"Now, when my stomach starts rumbling, someone *really* needs help getting rid of the grouchies. Why don't you tell me what the problem is."

Sally told Grumpy Bear how she had started to
be afraid of the dark and how she felt grumpy all day
because she had gotten almost no sleep the night
before.

"Oh, Grumpy Bear," she
said. "I'm afraid that the same
thing will happen tonight. What
if I can't get to sleep again?"
Grumpy Bear gave her a very
ungrumpy smile and said, "Don't
worry about a thing Sally. I have a
friend who lives in the same place
that I do, the land of Care-a-lot,
and I'll bet he can help you
with your problem."
"Really?" asked Sally.
"Really," said Grumpy Bear.

"Now," he said, "you just go home, and be on the lookout for Bedtime Bear when you go to sleep tonight."

Then Grumpy Bear sailed up into the branches of the tree and was gone.

Sally felt better after talking to Grumpy Bear.
She wondered if Bedtime Bear would really help her.
That night Sally's mother finished reading her a
bedtime story. Then her mother switched off the light.
She said, "Sweet dreams," and left.

Sally was alone. She lay in the bed and looked at the dark. What was that white shape in the corner? Where was Bedtime Bear?

Sally flipped on her light and called for her father and asked, "Can I have a drink of water?"

"Of course you can," answered Sally's father, "but then you will have to go to sleep."

After Sally's father brought her the water, he said, "Sweet dreams," and switched off the light.

Sally flipped on the light again, called for her mother and asked, "Can I have a good night kiss?"

Sally's mother smiled. "Of course you can." She kissed Sally. Then she said, "Sweet dreams," and switched off the light.

"Well, first of all I want to show you that there is
nothing to be afraid of. See, your lamp and your doll
are just like they always were. It was only that your
eyes were playing tricks on you."

"Now I see," said Sally.

"All right then. Lie down, close those pretty eyes, and I'll get to work."

Sally turned her cheek into her pillow, scrunched her knees up into her chest, and Bedtime Bear sang her a lullaby.

Now Sally had been given everything that she needed; a bedtime story, a drink of water, and a good night kiss. But all that was not enough. It was dark, and Sally didn't like it. The dark wasn't cozy. It wasn't friendly.

In the dark Sally's pretty lamp didn't look so pretty.

In the dark Sally's wonderful doll didn't look so wonderful.

Where *was* that Bedtime Bear? Sally was starting to feel scared again.

All of a sudden something landed on her bed!
Sally sat right up, and there at the end of the bed
was a bear with a moon on its tummy!

"Are you Bedtime Bear?" Sally asked.
The bear winked and said, "You bet your buttons I am. Grumpy Bear sent me."

"Do you really live in a place called Care-a-lot?"

"Right you are. At least that's where I live during the day, but just remember that when the moon comes peeking in your window at night, I'm usually around somewhere making sure that someone gets a good night's sleep.

"Now I know that you are starting to feel afraid of the dark, but I think I can help you, if that's all right with you."

"I'd love it," Sally said.

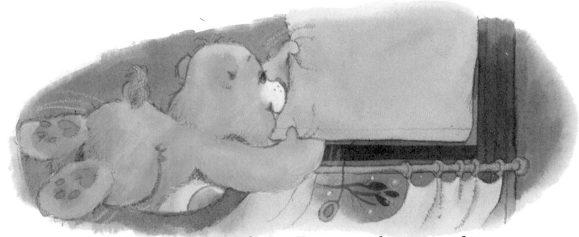

While he sang, Bedtime Bear was busy working. He stopped the window shades from making sharp, rattly sounds.

He stopped the curtains from making soft, whispery sounds.

He stopped the clock from making loud, ticking sounds. And Sally fell asleep.

The next day Sally really felt good.
At breakfast she smiled at her father.

In school she spelled every word correctly, and she and Amy made up and were friends again.

That night when it was time for bed, Sally hopped right under the covers. She told her father that she did not need a drink of water. She told her mother that she did not need a bedtime story.

"Just give me a good night kiss and switch off the light," she said. Sally was hoping that she would see Bedtime Bear again.

"Sweet dreams," said Sally's father.

"Sweet dreams," said Sally's mother.

Then they both left the room.

While she waited for Bedtime Bear, Sally looked
around her room.

Tonight her pretty lamp looked as pretty as it
always did.

Tonight her wonderful doll looked as wonderful as
it always did.

Sally knew that she wasn't afraid of the dark any
more.

Sally started to get sleepy. She tried
to keep awake for Bedtime Bear, but
her eyes gently closed.

Later that night Sally opened her eyes.
Was she dreaming? There, standing on a
beautiful cloud, each holding a twinkling
star, were Grumpy and Bedtime Bear.
They looked down at her.

Sally smiled sleepily. "Tuck me in;
tuck me in tight," she murmured.

And as she got comfortable, Sally
closed her eyes and dreamed a special
dream about the land of Care-a-lot.